# THE HAPPY PRINCE

# THE HAPPY PRINCE

FROM THE FAIRY TALE BY OSCAR WILDE

## JANE RAY

Dutton Children's Books

New York

*For Joseph, my own little Happy Prince*

J.R.

Illustrations copyright © 1994 by Jane Ray

*CIP Data is available.*

First published in the United States 1995 by Dutton Children's Books,
a division of Penguin Books USA Inc.
375 Hudson Street, New York, New York 10014

Originally published in Great Britain 1994 by Orchard Books, London
Typography by Amy Berniker
Printed in Belgium
First American Edition
ISBN 0-525-45367-9
1 3 5 7 9 10 8 6 4 2

**H**igh above the city, on a tall column, stood the statue of the Happy Prince. He was gilded all over with thin leaves of fine gold. For eyes he had two bright sapphires, and a large red ruby glowed on his sword hilt.

One night there flew over the city a little Swallow. He saw the statue on the tall column. So he alighted just between the feet of the Happy Prince.

"I have a golden bedroom," he said to himself, and he prepared to go to sleep; but just as he was putting his head under his wing, a large drop of water fell on him.

Then another drop fell. A third drop fell, and he looked up.

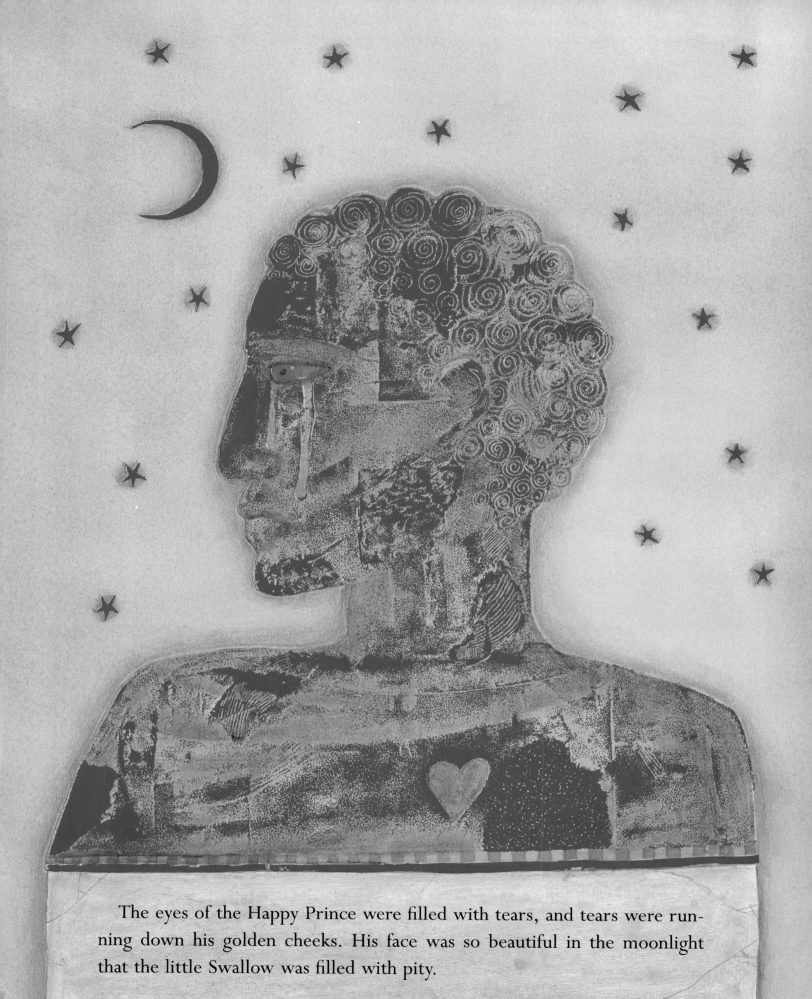

The eyes of the Happy Prince were filled with tears, and tears were running down his golden cheeks. His face was so beautiful in the moonlight that the little Swallow was filled with pity.

"Who are you?" he said.

"I am the Happy Prince."

"Why are you weeping then?" asked the Swallow. "You have quite drenched me."

"When I was alive and had
a human heart," answered the statue, "I did not know what tears were. Round
the garden ran a lofty wall, but I never cared to ask what lay beyond it,
everything about me was so beautiful. My courtiers called me the
Happy Prince. So I lived, and so I died. And now that I am dead
they have set me up here so high that I can see all the ugliness
and all the misery of my city, and though my heart is
made of lead yet I cannot choose but weep."

"Far away," continued the statue, "is a poor house. In a bed a little boy is lying ill. He is asking for oranges. His mother has nothing to give him but river water, so he is crying. Swallow, little Swallow, will you not bring her the ruby out of my sword hilt?"

"I am waited for in Egypt," said the Swallow. "My friends are flying up and down the Nile, and talking to the lotus flowers. Soon they will go to sleep in the tomb of the great King. The King is there himself in his

painted coffin. Round his neck is a chain of pale green jade, and his hands
are like withered leaves."

"Swallow, Swallow, little Swallow," said the Prince, "will you not stay
here with me for one night and be my messenger?"

The Happy Prince looked so sad that the little Swallow picked out the great ruby from the Prince's sword and flew away with it in his beak over the roofs of the town.

He passed by the cathedral tower, where the white marble angels were sculptured. He passed over the river and saw the lanterns hanging to the masts of the ships. At last he came to the poor house and laid the great ruby on the table.

Then he flew back to the Happy Prince and told him what he had done. "It is curious, but I feel quite warm now, although it is so cold."

When the moon rose the next day, the Swallow looked up at the Happy
Prince. "I am just starting for Egypt," he cried.

"Swallow, Swallow, little Swallow, will you not stay with me one night
longer?"

"I am waited for in Egypt," answered the Swallow. "There, on a great granite throne sits the God Memnon. All night long he watches the stars, and when the morning star shines he utters one cry of joy, and then he is silent. At noon the yellow lions come down to the water's edge to drink."

"Swallow, Swallow, little Swallow," said the Prince, "far away across the city I see a young man in a garret. He is trying to finish a play for the Director of the Theater, but he is too cold to write any more."

"I will wait with you one night longer," said the Swallow, who really had a good heart. "Shall I take him another ruby?"

"Alas! I have no ruby now," said the Prince. "My eyes are all that I have left. They are made of rare sapphires from India. Pluck out one of them and take it to him."

"Dear Prince," said the Swallow, "I cannot do that," and he began to weep.

"Swallow, Swallow, little Swallow," said the Prince, "do as I command you."

So the Swallow plucked out the Prince's eye and flew away to the student's garret. And when the student looked up he found the beautiful sapphire lying on his desk.

"I must bid you good-bye," cried the Swallow, when the moon rose the next night. "I am going to Egypt!"

"Swallow, Swallow, little Swallow," said the Prince, "will you not stay with me one night longer?"

"It is winter," answered the Swallow, "and the snow will soon be here. In Egypt the sun is warm on the palm trees, and the crocodiles lie in the mud and look lazily about them. Dear Prince, I must leave you, but next spring I will bring you back two beautiful jewels in place of those you have given away."

"In the square below," said the Happy Prince, "there stands a little match-girl. She has let her matches fall in the gutter. She has no shoes or stockings, and her little head is bare. Pluck out my other eye and give it to her."

"I will stay with you for one night longer," said the Swallow, "but I cannot pluck out your eye. You would be quite blind then."

"Swallow, Swallow, little Swallow," said the Prince, "do as I command you."

So the Swallow plucked out the Prince's other eye, darted down with it, and slipped the jewel right into the palm of the little match-girl's hand.

Then the Swallow came back to the Prince. "You are blind now," he said, "so I will stay with you always."

All the next day he sat on the Prince's shoulder and told him stories of what he had seen in strange lands. He told him of the red ibises, who stand in long rows on the banks of the Nile and catch goldfish in their beaks;

of the Sphinx, who is as old as the world itself and lives in the desert and knows everything;

of the great green snake that sleeps in a palm tree;

and of the King of the Mountains of the Moon, who is as black as ebony
and worships a large crystal.

"Dear little Swallow," said the Prince, "you tell me of marvelous things, but more marvelous than anything is the suffering of men and of women. There is no Mystery so great as Misery. Fly over my city, little Swallow, and tell me what you see there."

So the Swallow flew over the great city, and saw the rich making merry in their beautiful houses while the beggars were sitting at the gates. He flew into dark lanes and saw the white faces of starving children looking out listlessly at the black streets.

Then he flew back and told the Prince what he had seen.

"I am covered with fine gold," said the Prince. "You must take it off, leaf by leaf, and give it to the poor."

Leaf after leaf of the fine gold the Swallow picked off, till the Happy Prince looked quite dull and gray. Leaf after leaf of the fine gold he brought to the poor, and the children's faces grew rosier, and they laughed and played games in the street.

Then the snow came, and after the snow came the frost. Everybody went about in furs, and the little boys wore scarlet caps and skated on the ice.

The poor little Swallow grew colder and colder, but he would not leave the Prince. He loved him too well.

But at last the Swallow knew that he was going to die. "Good-bye, dear Prince!" he murmured. And he kissed the Happy Prince and fell down dead at his feet.

At that moment a curious crack sounded inside the statue. The leaden heart had snapped right in two. It certainly was a dreadfully hard frost.

Early the next morning the Mayor was walking in the square below with the Town Councillors. "Dear me! How shabby the Happy Prince looks!" he said. "And here is actually a dead bird at his feet!" he continued. "We must really issue a proclamation that birds are not allowed to die here."

So they pulled down the statue of the Happy Prince. Then they melted the statue in a furnace. But the broken heart would not melt, so it was thrown on a dust heap, where the dead Swallow was also lying.

"Bring me the two most precious things in the city," said God to one of his angels; and the angel brought him the leaden heart and the dead bird.

"You have rightly chosen," said God, "for in my garden of Paradise this little bird shall sing and the Happy Prince shall live for evermore."

$15.99

| DATE | | | |
|---|---|---|---|
| | | | |
| | | | |
| | | | |
| | | | |
| | | | |
| | | | |
| | | | |
| | | | |
| | | | |
| | | | |
| | | | |
| | | | |